MAGIC

Gemma

Amazon
Adventure

Written by De-ann Black
Illustrated by Malcolm Stokes

HENDERSON
PUBLISHING LTD

Contents

1. The Shadow People

"Gemma! Gemma! Are you up there?" called Mum impatiently from the hallway, as she wrapped her dripping wet hair in a towel. "It's Lucy on the phone. She wants some help with her History homework."

Oh not now! thought Gemma, who was deep in concentration, reading one of the history books she had borrowed from the school library. Carefully putting the book aside for the moment, she shouted, "Okay! I'm just coming!" and jumped off her bed. Running down the stairs, she picked up the receiver which Mum handed to her before disappearing back into the bathroom.

"Hello Lucy, what's the problem?" said Gemma brightly, knowing that History was something that Lucy absolutely hated and would do her utmost to get out of if she possibly could. They started talking about Mrs Storey's latest homework assignment – a project on ancient tribes and customs in the Amazon. Lucy, as Gemma had expected, was phoning her up to moan and groan about it. The twenty-minute, one-way conversation was punctuated only by the odd sympathetic murmur from Gemma, who had long since despaired of ever getting her friend to share her love of the subject. At last, with a sigh of relief, she replaced the handset and padded back to her room, anxious to pick up where she had left off.

"Phew!" she said, as she pressed her back to the door and closed it gently behind her. "Now, where was I?" Settling herself on the floor with a large notepad and her favourite pen, Gemma began to look through the pile of magazines and books which littered the carpet. Reaching distractedly for a chocolate biscuit, which she found was essential for the purposes of concentration, she picked up the book that she had been reading before she was so rudely interrupted.

"Secrets of the Amazon!" she whispered in between munches, reading the title of the big red book out loud and heaving it on to her lap. "I'm sure I'll find something exciting in here that I can use in my project."

As she turned over the smooth pages, Gemma breathed in their musty scent. They smelled old and well-read, and the type was in print much smaller than Gemma was used to. It reminded her of the books that her grandpa kept on his bookshelf. She pored over the colourful photographs of Amazonian birds and animals, flicking fascinatedly from jaguars to parrots. Then, pausing at one particular chapter she was intrigued to see the heading *Jewel of the Jungle*.

"I wonder what this is about?" she said. Skimming through the chapter, she found, to her delight, that it was all about a strange jewel which was reported to have gone missing. The more she read, the more intrigued she became, especially when she discovered that the jewel was in fact a sacred ruby belonging to an Amazonian tribe called the Shadow People. She studied the pictures of the tribe, and looked at their faces, which were painted with bright colours, their necks adorned with colourful necklaces. "The Shadow People were a secretive tribe, who believed in the mystic power of the phantom jaguar..." Gemma read on. This creature, she discovered, was meant to haunt the jungle. She looked again at the photographs and was captivated by the pictures of the tribespeople with thin reeds stuck in the sides of their noses like whiskers, making them look like ferocious jaguars.

The story explained that the Shadow People worshipped in a magnificent temple, hidden deep in the heart of the jungle, which was guarded by a stone jaguar statue. The eyes of the jaguar were inset with topaz gemstones, giving the animal a fierce, fiery-gold stare. Gemma traced her fingers around the picture of the statue, and shivered as the eyes seemed to glare penetratingly back at her. Then she carried on reading softly to herself, so that she didn't miss any of the detail.

"The jaguar had a mystical third eye set

in its forehead, which supposedly gave it the power to see into the unknown. This third eye was a large ruby known as the Jewel of the Jungle and in 1933 it was stolen."

Gemma gazed again at the jaguar illustration and imagined it creeping stealthily through the jungle undergrowth, padding through the mists, unseen and unheard. It certainly looks scary enough to frighten away strangers, she thought, but I wonder who was daring enough to steal the jewel in the first place?

Turning to the last page she read differing theories. The most convincing one to her was that it was stolen by hunters, but this theory couldn't be proved because the jewel had never been recovered.

"Wow! What a great story!" she sighed to herself. "How can Lucy say that History's boring when it's got stories like this to tell."

Dreamily, she left the book and thought about what she'd read. "I wish I could go back to 1933," she sighed, "and meet the Shadow People. Maybe I could find their precious ruby!"

The soft light of her reading lamp was beginning to make Gemma feel drowsy. Leaving the books in a pile, she lay on her bed and closed her eyes. She yawned contentedly, images of jaguars and strange temples recurring in her mind.

Later that evening, she awoke with a start. "What time is it?" she muttered, fumbling for her watch. Outside, a dazzling flash of lightning lit up the night sky. It was so bright that it woke her cat, Geronimo. He had been curled up, fast asleep on a cushion in his favourite chair near the window. Leaping from the chair, he hid under Gemma's bed. Gemma bent down and lifted the edge of the duvet to check that he was all right. Two topaz eyes, wide with fear, peered out at her.

"It's best you stay there until the storm is over," Gemma told him. She reached underneath and gave his soft, ginger fur a reassuring pat. As she did so, her fingers brushed against the familiar shape of the small wooden jewellery box which she kept hidden there.

"I haven't seen you for a while," she said, and pulled the box towards her.

Geronimo purred, spreading himself out in the extra space.

Lifting the box carefully on to her lap, Gemma gently opened the lid. Beneath the everyday baubles that she'd 'borrowed' from her mum's ever-expanding collection lay her secret necklaces. No one else in the world had necklaces as special as these – they were mysteriously powerful... strangely magical. Since she had first discovered them hidden in a cave when she was on holiday in Cornwall, Gemma's life had changed. Now, incredibly, she seemed to have the ability to travel through time! She hadn't told anybody about the jewellery – not even Lucy. No, this was her secret and she didn't want to spoil it. As she pored over the necklaces, one in particular caught her eye. It was made out of carved and polished wooden beads, just like a type of tribal necklace. Picking it up, she gazed at the warm grain of the wood and ran the beads through her fingers. Would the necklace have the power to whisk her off to the Amazon in search of the ruby jewel, she wondered. Gemma stood for a moment, holding the necklace, and imagined what it would really be like to go there. She'd always loved reading about the Amazon and its people in her dad's pile of National Geographic magazines. "I wonder if it would be possible..." she mused as she fastened the wooden beads around her neck. As she did so she could hear a voice in her head, chanting,

You shall journey far and wide
Across Time's endless seas...

And as the voice chanted, Gemma felt herself falling down, down, down, down...

"Oops!" Gemma exclaimed, almost losing her balance as her feet slipped on what appeared to be thick vines. Looking down she could see that her bedroom carpet was gone, replaced instead by a maze of roots littered with fallen leaves and twigs. A huge leaf from a tropical plant swatted her in the face.

There was no need to wonder if the magic necklace had worked; this was the jungle all right! The sights, sounds and scent of it surrounded her for as far as the eye could see. It was thick with trees and beautiful tropical greenery, and the air felt heavy with moisture. Strange animal sounds echoed in the distance, and Gemma shivered with a mixture of excitement and anticipation.

"I'm here," she whispered to herself nervously. "I've done it!"

Taking a deep breath she paused for a moment to think about what she should do first. Screwing up her eyes so that they grew accustomed to the dim light, she glanced around, hoping to see a path through the trees, but there was nothing – nothing but tropical plants and ferns, broken up by the odd splash of bright red flowers. Phew! It's so hot here! she thought to herself, instinctively wiping her forehead with her hand. The climate was humid, and the air smelled of a lush mixture of tropical plants and exotic fruits.

Which direction should I take? she wondered – it would be so easy to get lost.

Just then, the faraway cry of some Amazonian creature sent a shiver down Gemma's spine, and she sensed a danger in the air, as if she was being watched.

No sooner had this thought crossed her mind, than she heard a strange rustling sound coming from...she wasn't certain where...it seemed to be coming from all directions.

Her heart began to beat anxiously and she could feel her hands growing clammy with nerves. What if she was being stalked by a wild animal; what should she do? Now stay calm, she told herself firmly. Don't panic and you'll be fine.

The long branches of an enormous tree dangled above her head like skinny arms. Looking up, Gemma considered climbing the tree and staying there safely until whatever was lurking in the bushes went away.

But at that moment, just as she was about to reach up and grab hold of a branch, several men like the tribespeople from her book appeared before her.

Gemma jumped with fright, realising that she had rapidly become surrounded.

The men wore colourful tribal clothes and carried long spears which they pointed straight at Gemma.

Her heart sank and she could feel a lump rising to her throat. How can I explain that I've come from the future, and that I want to help them find the Jewel of the Jungle? she asked herself nervously. How will they ever understand me?

"You...you must be the Shadow People," she heard herself say – although she couldn't believe that she'd actually managed to say anything at all. The warriors stared at her. Gemma swallowed hard.

Maybe if I mention the ruby, she thought hopefully, then they'll see that I'm friendly.

Taking a deep, steadying breath, she added, "I know about your jewel – the Jewel of the Jungle – being stolen, and I'd like to try to help you find it – if...if you'll let me."

Lowering their spears, the men exchanged

looks, clearly surprised that she knew about their sacred jewel.

Gemma breathed a huge sigh of relief. They seemed to understand what she was saying, although they didn't look very friendly. Their faces were painted with a white band across the cheekbones, and thin reeds stuck out from the sides of their noses, giving them a fierce, cat-like appearance. Their hair was blue-black and their skin was a rich copper colour.

One of the men stepped closer to Gemma and studied her curiously. He must be the chief, she thought, because he wore more feathers and beads than the others.

Standing perfectly still, she let him take a good long look at her.

Judging by his baffled expression, he had never seen a twelve-year-old girl like her before! Her clothes – especially her trainers, which he prodded with the tip of his spear – seemed to fascinate him. She could sense his bewilderment. The other men were equally curious, and eyed her suspiciously.

"I can explain," Gemma said, giving the chief a friendly smile, although she knew that her arrival and bizarre appearance were going to take more than a little explaining.

"My name is Gemma. Gemma James," she revealed. "I think you should know that I know about the hunters – "

"Hunters!" the chief said angrily. He glared straight at Gemma. "You belong to the hunters?"

"Oh no, I'm er..." Gemma stammered, momentarily lost for words. "I know about them stealing your ruby – the third eye of the stone jaguar."

Several of the tribesmen grumbled and began thumping the end of their spears impatiently on the ground.

Gemma looked around at them. "I'm not a hunter. You must believe me. I'm here alone."

Just then, the spear thumping grew respectfully quiet as another tribesman stepped forward and approached Gemma. She noticed that he looked slightly different from the others, having a vivid blue band painted across his cheeks.

Thinking back to the stories she had read about tribes in the jungle, she wondered if he might be the medicine man. He was wearing several wooden necklaces around his neck, similar to her own, which she thought might be a sign that he was well-respected within the community. Rather than carrying a spear, he held a colourful, carved bamboo rod which made a distinct rattling sound.

Uncannily, when she looked at him, Gemma didn't feel quite as scared. Was she imagining it, or were his eyes not quite so threatening? Her instincts had often proved right in the past, so she mentally crossed her fingers that she could trust him.

"Why are you here?" he questioned in a low whisper.

Perhaps he might understand the truth if she dared tell him, but before she had a chance to explain, the chief's thunderous voice shook her to her bones.

"Take her!" he roared, his angry eyes regarding her distrustfully.

Two of the men grabbed hold of her. Gemma was trapped. She had no choice but to follow the chief, who was striding on ahead.

"Where are you taking me?" Gemma shouted, struggling unsuccessfully to break free. No answer was given. Her voice rang through the trees and then silence fell again.

Panic flashed through her mind as the

adow People led her against her will through the hot, sticky jungle. Gemma was having second thoughts. This definitely wasn't what she had planned. Perhaps it had been a mistake coming to the Amazon after all, but it was too late to worry about that now. Her main concern was to escape – and fast!

2. Morgan's Logbook

Escape was impossible, Gemma realised ...or at least for the moment. She trudged resignedly through the sweltering jungle.

"It's so hot!" she sighed, wiping the sweat from her brow. The heat reminded her of the time she had gone on holiday to the Caribbean with her parents, her brother Simon and sister Katie. Gemma was the only one in her family who hadn't suffered from sunstroke or prickly heat – a fact she was very proud of. Right now, all she could think about was an ice-cold can of coke. Her throat was parched; she swallowed and then coughed dryly.

The medicine man, whose name she had learned was Ituxi, told her that she was being taken to the Shadow People's village. Gemma walked on, trying to work out what she was going to say when she got there. I don't know what I'm afraid of most, she thought privately – being captured by the Shadow People, or finding myself alone here in the jungle at the mercy of who knows what.

"What was that?" she gasped, suddenly seeing the shadow of a large cat loom ahead of them in the bushes. She only caught a glimpse of it; one moment it was there, the next it had vanished. "It looked like a jaguar."

Ituxi was walking beside her and instinctively she moved closer to him as if seeking his protection.

"There are no jaguars in this part of the jungle," he said knowledgeably. "None that are alive anyway."

Gemma's eyes widened. "Are you suggesting it was a ghost?"

"There are only two jaguars here," he explained as they walked along. "One of them is the stone jaguar which guards our temple – and the other is the phantom jaguar which stalks the valley."

Gemma swallowed hard. "And stone jaguars don't prowl around in the bushes, right?"

Ituxi nodded, and smiled slightly at her comment.

"I'm not sure whether I believe in ghosts and spooky superstitions," she remarked, trying to sound brave, but shivering at the possibility that she might have just seen a ghost.

"The jungle is filled with superstitions," he said in a low voice. "It is safer to believe in the unknown than to discount it," he added wisely.

"Oh, I believe in lots of strange things," she confessed. "And I certainly believe in magic."

"What kind of magic?" he asked, intrigued by her comment.

Gemma touched the wooden beads around her neck. This was her chance to explain to Ituxi how she got there. She sensed that she could trust him, and spoke in a whisper so only he could share her secret. "The kind of magic that can take you to weird and wonderful places; to faraway lands and distant worlds."

A knowing look passed between them, and she hoped that he was beginning to understand. "My magic necklace brought me to the jungle," she whispered.

Ituxi's eyes flashed curiously as he tried to grasp what she was saying.

"Why did you come here?" he said in a hushed tone.

"I've come to try to help you find the stolen ruby," she whispered. "If the hunters have it, maybe I can help you get it back from them."

He shook his head. "We tried to capture them at the temple, but they managed to escape us. By now they will be long gone."

Gemma pondered for a moment. Then she had an idea. "Maybe not. What if they plan to return in order to steal more treasures?"

He looked thoughtful. "Well, I suppose it's possible, but – "

"Ituxi, you have said enough!" the chief bellowed, effectively silencing any further conversation before they reached the village.

Never mind, Gemma thought to herself; at least Ituxi understands why I'm here – and best of all, he seems willing to be my friend.

The Shadow People's village was hidden deep within the heart of the jungle, disguised by the wilderness of trees which made it almost invisible to outsiders. It was protected on one side by a mountain, which was so high that it blotted out a huge expanse of sky. The village was small in comparison, and seemed to be crouching down, hiding out of sight within the shadow of the mountain.

A vine-covered archway, carved from a giant rock, led into the centre of the village.

Gemma was fascinated by what she saw – imagine if Dad could see this, she thought to herself. Everywhere was so naturally beautiful. The houses were built from a mixture of bamboo and dried clay, and covered with lots of greenery to make them blend into their surroundings. Each one had an overhanging roof made out of thatch.

At the far end of the settlement, a waterfall gushed down the mountain side and poured into a deep, sparkling pool. She could see many of the villagers collecting water in clay pots, and children were happily splashing about in the shallows.

The sound of the children's laughter ceased abruptly as Gemma was led into their midst. Everyone stopped their business to stare at her. No wonder they're surprised, Gemma thought, realising how outlandish she must appear to them. Many of the younger children seemed frightened of her, and clung tightly to their parents.

If only they knew how scared I am, Gemma sighed, wondering what was going to happen next.

Moments later, two warriors led her into

a small round hut near the edge of the waterfall, while the chief, whose name Gemma discovered was Dandano, called his people to the centre of the village to explain about their unusual visitor.

Food and water were brought to Gemma, but the warriors kept guard outside the hut door, preventing her escape.

Inside, she sat on the dry, dusty ground, gazing up at the circle of daylight which streamed in through a hole in the roof.

There were no windows, and it took a few moments for her eyes to adjust to the darkness. It was so hot that she gratefully drank all the water she had been given in three thirsty gulps.

"This is one adventure I'm never likely to forget," Gemma mused to herself, hoping that there weren't any nasty insects crawling around. Things were bad enough without jungle creepy-crawlies!

Her eyes grew accustomed to the dim light, and she could see the inside of the hut more clearly. There was no furniture, but she noticed something breaking the shaft of sunlight on the ground opposite her.

Wondering what it was, she got up and went over to take a closer look. She carefully poked the small, dusty object with her toe, fearing it might be something horrible, then quickly realised that it was a book. She sat down again in the centre of the hut, so that she could scrutinise it under the light filtering through the roof.

Resting the battered cover on her outstretched hand, Gemma turned the pages one by one. To her amazement, she found that the book was some sort of logbook, and it belonged to a man called Zack Morgan. Judging by what it said,

Morgan was a ruthless man. As she studied the scrawled writing more slowly, Gemma's eyes opened wide. Morgan was the ringleader of the hunters!

She read fast and furiously – here was his very own detailed record of how he planned to steal the sacred ruby! He had even noted down that he intended to rob the Shadow People of the small but precious gem-studded statues which the tribe kept within their temple.

Before she had the chance to read any more, she heard Ituxi's voice instructing the two warrior guards to stand aside and let him in to talk to her.

Forgetting herself for an instant, Gemma said, "Have you read this?" She thrust the logbook at him the moment he stepped inside the hut.

"What is it?"

"It's Zack Morgan's logbook...a sort of diary...describing in detail how he stole the Jewel of the Jungle. Morgan seems to be the ringleader of the hunters."

Ituxi was confounded. "Where did you find this?"

She pointed to the floor of the hut.

Before he could work out how the logbook had got there, a young voice interrupted them from the open doorway.

"I can explain everything, father," said a boy. Gemma looked across at him. He was quite tall, with the build of a swimmer – broad shoulders tapering to a slim waist, and strong, lean limbs. His shiny, midnight-coloured hair was long and unruly, and his eyes sparkled mischievously. She guessed that he was about thirteen years old, and could see that he bore a striking resemblance to his father.

"Come inside, Tal," Ituxi said. Then he turned to Gemma. "You can trust him – and you can trust me."

Gemma nodded her understanding. Now she had two new friends on her side.

The boy stepped in and closed the door behind him. She could see that he was trying his best not to stare at her, although he couldn't help the occasional glance in her direction.

"Do you know where this book came from?" Ituxi asked his son.

"I found it near the temple this morning," the boy explained. "The hunters must have dropped it. I hid it here until you got back to the village." He paused and shot a begrudging glance at Gemma. "I didn't expect anyone else to find it first."

"Well, maybe it's just as well I did," she explained, "because it's clear from this logbook that Morgan and his men are planning to go back to the temple to steal your other treasures."

Tal nodded. "Yes, you're right. The book says the hunters will return."

Gemma put forward a tentative suggestion. "If you let me go, I'll try to help you get your ruby back from Zack Morgan."

Ituxi smiled gently at her. "But you're just a girl, not a warrior. What can you possibly do?"

"I can get into Morgan's camp. He won't suspect that I'm helping your tribe, and hopefully I'll be able to win his trust long enough to get my hands on the ruby."

"But we don't know where the hunters are camped," Ituxi reasoned.

"It's bound to mention it here," she said

excitedly, quickly flicking through the logbook. "Yes, here it is – it says that they intend setting up camp..." she hesitated as she read the location, "at the far side of the Valley of the Phantom Jaguar – a dense, unfathomable forest and swamp, feared by Amazonian tribes."

Gemma's heart sank. Of all the places in the jungle, Morgan would have to choose camp creepy!

"I'm not afraid," Tal announced confidently.

"It's too dangerous," his father replied.

"Morgan knows he's safe there," the boy argued. "He probably thinks no one would dare go to the haunted valley – especially not at night."

"That's true," Ituxi agreed, reconsidering the idea.

"Look, father, I know the valley well," Tal continued. "I could lead Gemma to the camp and make sure she arrives safely."

His father nodded. "Do you remember where the canoes are hidden? You'll need them to cross the Skeleton Swamp."

Gemma held up her hands in horror.

"Wait a minute! I don't mind helping you, but I'm not so sure about all this spooky stuff – phantom jaguars, haunted valleys and now skeleton swamps – particularly at night. Can't we at least go while it's daylight?"

Father and son looked up at the circle of azure sky peering in through the roof. "By the time you swim through the waterfall, darkness will have fallen," Ituxi told her. "But you don't have to worry, the jungle is never completely dark. The fireflies will keep you company."

"Swim through the waterfall!" she repeated, astounded.

The boy shrugged his shoulders. "It's the only way out of the village without being seen."

"If you wait another day, you won't need to escape," said Ituxi. "That's what I came to tell you. Dandano has decided to take you to the nearest missionary settlement tomorrow. He thinks your presence here might cause trouble for the tribe, but he wants no harm to come to you, so he has suggested that you are taken to your own kind of people. They will look after you."

Gemma grimaced. "No way am I going to the missionaries!" she protested. "Besides, my magic only lasts for two days at the most, so I don't have any time to waste in the jungle."

Ituxi was fascinated. "What happens when your magic runs out?"

"I go back home where I came from." Tal stared at her in disbelief.

"So, will you go to the Valley of the Phantom Jaguar with my son?" Ituxi prompted her. "He is our best young warrior, and I will travel with both of you as far as the Skeleton Swamp. Then I must return and talk to Dandano. I will try to persuade him that the hunters will return, and that we must defend the temple."

Reluctantly, Gemma agreed to go, but niggling at the back of her mind was one thought – just what had she let herself in for?

3. Through the Skeleton Swamp

Ituxi managed to distract the two guards so that Gemma and Tal could sneak out of the hut. He arranged to meet up with them later, at the edge of the haunted valley.

It was getting late and the villagers were in their homes. This was the ideal time to escape through the waterfall, when no one was looking.

"Hurry," Tal whispered, urging Gemma to keep up with him as they crept through the dense green foliage. "And remember to keep to the shadows so we won't be seen."

The noise of water rushing down the mountain side grew louder and louder. To Gemma it rumbled as ominously as thunder, and she tried hard to dismiss second thoughts about swimming through it. She was still reasoning with herself when they arrived at the edge of a glistening pool. Its shimmering green depths looked surprisingly inviting in the twilight. Keeping out of sight, Tal slipped nimbly into the bubbling water. Steeling herself, Gemma followed, swimming as silently as a crocodile. As they approached the waterfall, Tal raised his voice to make himself heard over the thunderous cascade. "There's a gap in the rock that we can swim through to reach the other side." He pointed beneath the surface to an opening in the sunken depths. "Take a deep breath and follow me," he shouted.

Taking two huge gulps of air, Gemma dived underwater. Swimming with her clothes on was difficult, but she mustered all her strength and followed her guide.

She could see Tal just ahead of her. Swimming as fast as she could to keep up with him, it wasn't long before she reached the middle of the waterfall where she could feel the water crashing down around her.

At that moment, to her relief, she found that they were through to the other side. They popped up like two corks, gasping for air.

Her clothes stuck to her like a second

skin as she climbed out of the water on to the grassy bank. Standing up, she squeezed the residue from her soaking wet hair, and squirmed at the sensation of her trainers squelching beneath her toes. Yuck!

Tal, who was wearing a loincloth, was already walking on ahead towards the edge of the forest which was silhouetted by the glow of a silvery-white moon. As she watched him, she couldn't help thinking how much he looked like Mowgli from *The Jungle Book*.

"My father said he'd meet us over here." Tal pointed in the direction of a grove of leafless black trees. The spiky branches stretched upwards like the fingers of a skeleton, clawing at the night sky.

"Peculiar looking trees," Gemma remarked, shuddering at the sight of them.

"They're petrified," he said, meaning that they were fossilised.

"So am I," she quipped, trying to make light of the situation.

Tal smiled at her. "There's no sign of my father yet," he said, as they reached the meeting point. "But I'm sure he'll be here soon."

Gemma sat down on a rock. "I don't mind waiting; it'll give me a chance to dry off."

Tal sat down opposite her, his eyes bright with curiosity. "Is that really a magic necklace you're wearing?"

Gemma raised her hand self-consciously to her throat and felt the beads beneath her fingers. "Yes...I found it. It's part of some secret treasure." He listened eagerly to her story.

"What do your family and friends think?" he asked, when she'd finished telling him.

She smiled, imagining their reaction. "Oh, I've never told them – they wouldn't believe me."

"I believe you," he said.

"Yes, but you live in the jungle – a place where magic is believable. I've been wondering...why are you called the Shadow People?"

"Watch this," he said, proceeding to demonstrate. Walking away from her, he seemed to melt into the night and disappear. Then, as if by magic, he re-appeared right before her eyes.

She smiled. "Oh, I get it – it's because you're good at playing hide and seek. Anyone can do that...just watch me!"

She ran into the trees and crouched down to hide, expecting him to discover her at any moment, but as the seconds ticked by she began to feel nervous. "Tal! Can you see me?" Nothing. Not a sound. Opening her eyes, she panicked.

"Tal, where are you?" she called out, her voice echoing through the eerie silence. She stood up again, forgetting about hide and seek in this scary place, and began searching for him. She was afraid that she might get lost if she ventured too far away, and Tal was nowhere to be seen. Oh, where on earth is he? she wondered anxiously.

"Hello! I'm here," came a voice from behind her.

Spinning round to face him, she felt the relief flood through her. "Where did you get to? You scared me, disappearing like that!"

He grinned at her mischievously. "I was walking in a wide circle around you."

She frowned. "I didn't hear you."

"That's the other reason we're called the Shadow People – shadows are silent...but it takes a long time to learn how to move through the jungle without making a sound."

"Well, thanks for warning me – I was beginning to think I'd got lost!" she said, giving him a playful slap on the shoulder.

At that moment, Ituxi arrived, taking them both by surprise. "I see you made it safely through the waterfall."

Gemma was glad to see him.

"I hope Tal hasn't been frightening you," he said to her.

"Oh no, he was just demonstrating how skilful he is at moving silently through the jungle."

Casting a meaningful look at the night sky, Ituxi said, "We must hurry while the moon is still bright."

"Erm...where exactly is the Valley of the Phantom Jaguar?" asked Gemma curiously.

"This way," replied Ituxi, pointing towards the depths of the ghostly forest.

With Tal on one side and Ituxi on the other, Gemma ventured apprehensively into the ghostly realms of the forest.

Her heart was in her mouth. "What happens if we come across the phantom jaguar?" she asked bluntly. "I mean, I've heard that ghosts can't do you any real harm. Is that true?"

Ituxi's expression was serious. "Many warriors have tried to hunt down the jaguar, but have later been found with their limbs torn to shreds by the cat's razor-sharp claws."

Gemma gulped in horror – me and my big mouth! she thought.

"Don't worry, I know a safe route through the forest," Ituxi reassured her.

"Have you ever seen the jaguar?" she asked him.

"Yes, I have seen its fiery eyes and have encountered its rage."

A shiver ran down Gemma's spine. "What happened?"

"It vanished into the night."

Tal offered an explanation. "It only

harms those who threaten its territory. Often it just watches from a distance."

"Well, let's hope it keeps away from us tonight," she muttered under her breath.

The further they ventured, the darker and creepier the forest became. The branches of the trees seemed to be linking arms high above them, creating archways which were so dense that no moonlight could get through.

"I can hardly see where we're going," she said, trying not to stray from Ituxi's side. Several times she tripped and almost fell over the twisted mass of vines which curled and writhed on the ground like venomous snakes beneath her feet.

"The swamp is just ahead of us," said Ituxi. "Not far now."

It was then that she heard a strange, fiendish sound coming from the edge of the trees – a sort of low, unearthly snarl.

"Did you hear that?" she gasped.

"Ssh!" Tal hissed. "We don't want to attract its attention."

Attract its attention! That's one way of putting it, thought Gemma. "I think it's already seen us," she whispered.

"Stay close to me," Ituxi murmured. "And whatever you do, don't look directly into its eyes."

"Why not?"

"Because it will try to steal your soul," he warned.

I don't believe I'm hearing this, thought Gemma, shivering to herself.

The Skeleton Swamp lay within sight. She could see its murky black water swirling in the gloom, shrouded in a low-lying, midnight mist.

The air was calm – so what was making the water ripple? She was tempted to glance over her shoulder, just to convince herself that they really were safe. From the corner of her eye, she glimpsed something prowling in the distance, but before she could make it out clearly she was relieved to see it turn away and disappear back into its twilight world.

"This is where I must leave you," Ituxi told her. "Tal will lead you the rest of the way. Trust him, he knows the jungle well."

"What about you?" she asked.

He smiled. "Don't worry, the phantom will never see me – I will disappear into the shadows."

Tal called over to Gemma, "I've found the canoes."

He was tugging them out from their hiding place beneath some bushes, so she went over to help him drag one towards the water. The ground was soft. It felt like she was squelching across fudge.

By the time she turned her attention back to Ituxi he had vanished.

"Come on, Gemma, we have to go," said Tal, ready and waiting in his dug-out canoe.

Climbing into her boat, she picked up the single wooden paddle which was lying on the bottom. She thought back to the time that she and Dad had gone canoeing on an outdoor adventure holiday, so that she could remember the basics of how to paddle. She was a bit wobbly at first, but she put that down to the fact that the boats, which were carved from tree trunks, weren't very steady.

"Where are we heading, Tal?"

"For the other side of the swamp. See those trees dangling in the water over there?"

She looked across at the trees, their long, willowy branches trailing down like a black lace veil. "Yes, I see them."

"That's where we're going. It isn't far."

The moon cast a luminous glow on the water, spotlighting Gemma and Tal as they paddled smoothly to their destination.

She scanned the swamp, suppressing a shudder. How creepy it looked – and she had the strangest feeling that they weren't alone.

"Does anyone live here?" she whispered quietly, feeling the need to keep her voice low.

"Only the souls of the skeletons."

She might have guessed that he'd say something like that! "Is there anything in this jungle that is still alive?"

Tal's gaze drifted to a log floating nearby. "That seems to be breathing," he murmured in a hushed tone.

Gemma's voice rose excitedly. "What is it?"

"Don't ask, just keep paddling."

"Is it a skeleton?"

"No, but I wish it was," he whispered.

4. Hunters' Hide-out

As they paddled ever closer, Gemma cried, "It's a crocodile!"

The log raised its head and stared at her with beady yellow eyes. Opening its huge jaws, it let out a vicious, throaty hiss.

"Stay calm," said Tal.

Stay calm! thought Gemma – you must be joking! She began canoeing crazily for the shore, heading straight for the dangling trees. No way was she prepared to be a sitting duck for some hungry crocodile, whatever Tal said. He had no choice but to follow in her wake.

Unfortunately, Gemma's furious paddling alerted several other crocodiles, and soon they found themselves surrounded, as though they were floating in a lethal reptile soup.

"This swamp is crawling with crocodiles," she shouted, struggling to make her way to the trees.

Tal was next to her now, paddling

cautiously but confidently through the water so as not to disturb the crocodiles more than Gemma had already.

Gemma was terrified that she wasn't going to make it.

"Stop splashing!" he shouted. "If you panic, so will they – and they'll go for us."

"It's all right for you – you're used to scaly monsters!" she retaliated, her heart racing.

Seconds later, a crocodile lunged into her canoe. She rocked and flailed, but could not stop herself from tumbling into the swamp. As the beast dragged the canoe down into the deep water, Gemma reached up and grabbed hold of a branch which was dangling overhead, pulling herself clear of the crocodile's jaws. Its teeth clicked as it snapped again at her heels, narrowly missing taking a bite out of her leg.

"Aargh! Help me, Tal!" she gasped, climbing higher to safety.

Tal reached the edge of the swamp and jumped from his canoe to land out of harm's way, on to the mushy ground. Gemma was clutching the branch, her face deathly pale, tears welling up in her eyes.

"You finally made it, then?" she called down to him crossly from her tree-top vantage point.

He waved up at her. "Yes, but you did fine on your own! We'd better get going – the swampland is dangerous."

Gemma raised her eyebrows and wiped her eyes frustratedly. "How much more dangerous can it possibly get?"

"Come on!" said Tal. "Let's get out of here – fast."

She had no option, so grabbing hold of the nearest vine, Gemma swung herself downwards. She had always wanted to swing through the jungle like they did in the movies, and now was her big chance. She'd practised rope-training in her gymnastics class and thought that she could handle this, no problem.

"Let go!" Tal shouted, clearly alarmed. "Let go now!"

"Don't worry, I won't fall," she cried confidently, soaring through the air.

"It's a *snake*!" he yelled at the top of his voice.

Her blood turned to ice, realising that this was no vine she'd grabbed hold of! Even worse was the thought of how big the snake might possibly be. Instinctively, Gemma let go and dropped to the ground. Tal stretched out a helping hand and pulled her to her feet. He was trying his best to hide his laughter, but she could see the smirk playing on his lips.

She looked at him indignantly. "What's so funny?"

He imitated her earlier remark, "How much more dangerous can it get?"

"Well, I didn't know it was a snake, did I?" she protested.

"Ssh!" He froze, listening intently to a slithering sound coming from the swamp.

"Run!" Tal shouted, grabbing hold of her hand to pull her in the right direction. Only when they were a safe distance away did they slow down.

"What was it?" she asked breathlessly.

"A giant swamp lizard."

Gemma shuddered. "I've had enough – all these reptiles give me the creeps."

"Speaking of reptiles – Morgan's camp

is over there."

Following his gaze, she saw the glow of campfires in the distance. The amber radiance rose up towards the starlit sky, pinpointing their hideaway.

Gemma and Tal pressed on, winding their way through the jungle, eager to reach the hunter's camp.

It was still dark when they arrived.

"I'll go in alone," Gemma whispered.

Tal looked concerned. "What will you tell the hunters?"

She smiled thoughtfully. "I thought I'd make up a story – something that will appeal to their greed."

"Be careful. If you need me, I won't be far away," he promised.

She turned around to look at the camp, planning her best route. Several tents were pitched around fires, which were undoubtedly lit to keep wild animals at bay.

The hunters will be surprised to see someone like me turn up out of the blue, she thought, hoping her story would be convincing.

When she turned back, Tal had disappeared into the shadows.

Taking a deep breath to steady her nerves, Gemma walked warily into the centre of the camp, guided by the glow of the fire light. Three men were on guard, and as soon as Gemma approached one of them alerted Morgan, who was asleep in his tent.

Gemma swallowed nervously. "Well, it's now or never," she told herself.

"Who are you, and what are you doing here?" Zack Morgan said gruffly, rubbing his eyes as he walked out of his tent. Although he had clearly just woken up, he was carrying a rifle and looked at her suspiciously.

"I'm sorry to disturb you – I've lost my way. When I saw the light from your campfire I headed straight for it," she lied.

"What are you doing in the jungle?" he snapped. "Didn't your parents ever warn you not to go out on your own?" Then, with a wink to his men, he added, "You never know what wild animals are hiding in the trees..."

Ignoring his remark, Gemma continued with her story. "I'm here with my father, but I wandered off and got lost in the swamp. We've come here with a group of explorers who are searching for a secret gold mine – "

At the mention of gold, Morgan's ears pricked up. Narrowing his eyes, he cut in abruptly, "What gold mine?"

"It's meant to be somewhere near a hidden temple."

"What do you know about the temple?"

"Oh, nothing much, but I do know there's a fortune in gold located very close to it. If you've got a map, I'll show you," she bluffed.

Morgan shouted to one of his men, "Jarrett, get me the map." Then, staring straight at her, he hissed, "You'd better not be lying to me."

Avoiding his eyes, Gemma gulped, kicking herself for suggesting that she could show him where the gold was.

"I'm telling you the truth," she insisted, inwardly panicking about how she was going to get out of showing him where her imaginary gold mine was on the map.

One of the hunters stood up for her.

"She's only a girl," he reasoned. "What harm can she possibly do?"

"I'll be the judge of that, Deakin," growled Morgan.

Jarrett hurried over with the map. Morgan snatched it from him and held it out for Gemma to read.

Map reading wasn't her best subject, and she hadn't a clue where the temple was anyway. She bit her lower lip, worried what to say. If she said the wrong thing, he would realise that she was lying, and goodness knows what he'd do then.

Morgan was fast becoming impatient with her. "The temple is here." He jabbed a finger at its location near the centre of the map. "So, where's the gold mine then?"

Sensing the menace in his voice, Gemma made a wild guess. "It's right there, just north of the temple," she announced, trying to sound convincing.

Morgan was thoughtfully silent.

She held her breath, waiting for his reaction, and wondered if she could escape if things turned nasty.

Finally, he spoke. "Few people have ever explored that area. It's so dense, no one knows for sure what's actually there."

Great! she shouted inwardly, trying to hide her smile. She'd picked an ideal reference point on the map – luck was on her side!

"Well, my father believes that's where

the gold is," she insisted.

He glared at her. "Is your father a fool?"

"No, he's not. He's very clever."

"Then why did he bring a young girl like you to this part of the world? No one in their right mind would do that."

She had to think fast. "Because there was nobody at home to take care of me ...and...I want to be an explorer when I grow up...besides, I'm handy to have around." Each reason on its own wasn't very strong, but she hoped that all three combined would convince him.

He sighed heavily, and Gemma took this as a sign that he believed her.

"Tomorrow, we're heading for the temple," he said.

I'll bet you are, Gemma thought darkly. You're going there to steal more treasures than you have already.

"Are you explorers, too?"

Morgan grinned, amused by her feigned innocence. "Yes, and you can travel with us if you like. We'll probably catch up with your father along the way. I'd be very interested to meet him."

I'm sure you would, thought Gemma, forcing a smile.

"But, if I discover you've been lying to me, you're in big trouble," he warned. She didn't doubt that for a second.

Without another word, he strode back towards his tent. "Bed down beside a fire for the night," he muttered over his shoulder. "And watch out for snakes," he added, sniggering to himself.

"Come on, I'll find you a blanket," Jarrett offered grudgingly.

Wrapping herself in the rough blanket and watching the flames dance in the fire, Gemma settled down to sleep. Instinct told her to stay awake, but she knew that she had to get some rest, or she would be in no fit state to steal the ruby away from Morgan. She was going to have to use all her wits and skill to beat him.

Next morning, the hunters rose at the crack of dawn. After breakfast, they packed their belongings into rucksacks, stamped out the dying embers of the fires, and headed straight for the temple.

The sun was already hot enough to scorch holes in the jungle mist, and the humidity was stifling. Trekking through the jungle was an arduous task. The men carried heavy rucksacks which slowed them down considerably, and Gemma was glad she didn't have to lug anything extra along with her.

During the journey, she listened to the men talking, hoping to discover where Morgan was hiding the ruby. She had noticed that he had a small leather pouch in the top pocket of his khaki jacket, and he kept checking to see if it was still safe. That must be the ruby's hiding place! He kept the map tucked in the back pocket of his trousers, and she considered stealing that, too. Without their map, the hunters would surely be lost.

At one point, Gemma overheard Jarrett and Deakin discussing the gold mine.

"Do you think the girl really knows what she's talking about?" asked Deakin.

Jarrett shrugged his shoulders. "She knew where the mine was on the map."

"Her father is with a group of

explorers," Deakin added. "Morgan reckons we should come across them near the hidden temple. There could be trouble."

"Only if they won't share the gold with us," Jarrett sneered. "Then they'll be sorry."

There was a pause in the conversation, then Jarrett made a personal observation about Gemma.

"The girl's clothes are a bit odd," he remarked.

Just then, Morgan shouted out an order. "Right men, take a break."

They halted in their tracks, shrugged off their rucksacks and sat down for a rest and a drink of water.

Morgan strode over to where Gemma sat. "Behaving yourself?"

"Of course," she replied, trying to sound bright, although she didn't feel it.

She was scared; Morgan was a horrible man. She wished that she could simply grab the ruby and the map right now and run away. To succeed, she'd have to wait for a chance to steal them when he least expected it.

5. The Bridge of No Return

Gemma and the hunters trekked deeper into the jungle. The dense vegetation closed in on them, swathing them in green. The humidity made Gemma's forehead damp with sweat, and her shirt was sticking to her skin. The men had to hack their way through the greenery using wide-bladed knives. It slowed their progress down considerably, but gave Gemma time to think about her next move.

She kept a close eye on Morgan, watching and waiting for a chance to steal the ruby.

"Give me your compass, Jarrett," Morgan barked. Jarrett handed it over.

Reading the map co-ordinates, he used the compass to check that they were heading in the right direction. "At this rate, we won't reach the temple until nightfall," he complained.

"We can't cut our way through any faster," Deakin snapped gruffly, wiping the sweat from his brow as he sliced at the undergrowth with his big knife. Several of the men grumbled in agreement with Deakin.

Morgan cursed under his breath, realising that there was nothing they could do to speed up the journey. He folded the map and jammed it into his trouser pocket. Then he checked the leather pouch again, to see if the ruby was still safe.

Gemma studied his every move.

"What are you staring at?" he growled at her.

"Nothing," she replied shakily.

He grabbed her roughly by the shoulders and shook her until her head felt dizzy.

"I've seen you watching me," he said angrily. "I know you're up to something, and when I figure it out, you'll be sorry."

"I'm not up to anything," she countered.

When he finally let go of her, she was trembling. Don't give in, she thought defiantly. Somehow, she had to find a way to outsmart him.

As she stumbled along, Gemma racked her brains for a solution to the problem. Obviously it wasn't safe to hang around near Morgan, and it would be virtually impossible to snatch the ruby from his jacket pocket.

While she was pondering what to do, she caught a glimpse of a shadow nearby. It was Tal, and he seemed to be warning her that something was about to happen.

At that moment there was a screeching sound, and a wild boar with vicious-looking tusks came rushing at them from the bushes, charging at full pelt. Gemma sprang out of the way and the hunters scattered, thrown into a panic.

Taking the rifle from his shoulder, Morgan aimed and fired a shot at the animal. He missed, but the sound scared it away temporarily.

Then the raging boar charged at them again. Jarrett tripped and stumbled to the ground, and the beast's tusks ripped open his rucksack. Morgan fumbled for a cartridge to reload his rifle.

Now was her chance – before fleeing, Gemma rushed forward and snatched the map from Morgan's pocket. He was so busy reloading that he didn't notice, but

Deakin saw her take it.

"She's stolen the map!" he shouted.

Without looking back, she raced towards the trees and the shadows where Tal was hiding, clutching the map tightly.

"Don't let her escape!" Morgan shouted furiously. "Stop her!"

Three of the hunters chased after her, leaving Morgan and the others to deal with the wild boar.

She raced off as fast as she could, the hunters in hot pursuit.

Tal was a few strides ahead and Gemma sprinted after him, the plants stinging her legs as she ran. Just when she thought that she was about to collapse from exhaustion, Tal stopped in front of her, and she realised that they had reached a bridge.

The bridge was made of ropes knotted together and it stretched across a fast-flowing river. To her dismay, Gemma noticed that the ropes were worn and frayed, and it didn't look to her as if the bridge could possibly support the weight of a girl, let alone a grown man. This is rapidly turning into an assault course, she thought to herself – somehow I just knew that the bridge would be old and tattered.

"Come on," Tal urged her. He climbed on to the bridge, arms stretched out holding the side ropes while he balanced step by step on the rope strands beneath his feet.

Gemma heard the sounds of the raging river far below.

"It doesn't look very safe," she said, hesitating at the brink. "Isn't there another route we can take?"

"No, there's no time, it's the only way," Tal called to her. By now he was a quarter of the distance across, and she could hear the shouts of the hunters getting nearer.

"Oh great – now I suppose I've got no option!" she muttered.

Taking a deep breath, Gemma tucked the map into her jeans pocket and gingerly stepped on to the bridge. It swayed from side to side, making it difficult for her to keep her balance.

"Pretend it's a gymnastics beam," she told herself calmly. "Look straight ahead, keep upright and try not to wobble."

Her technique seemed to work, and she made good progress across the bridge. She walked carefully, but presumed that if it had supported Tal's weight, it could easily hold her, too.

By the time Gemma had reached the middle of the bridge, Tal was safely on the other side. Well, if he can do it, so can I, she thought.

She tried not to listen to the sound of the river cascading furiously over the rocks. Don't look down, she urged herself, just keep going.

"There she is!" Jarrett shouted. "Don't let her get away. We need that map."

Gemma's heart leaped into her throat, and instinctively she glanced over her shoulder. She almost lost her balance as she turned to look in the hunters' direction, and she scrambled to steady her foothold on the rope again.

"Don't look at them," Tal shouted, "look at me. You're almost there now."

Nodding, she proceeded onwards, staring determinedly at him.

Behind, she could hear the hunters arguing about whether they should cross the bridge.

"Those ropes are ancient," one of them complained.

"I'm not putting a foot on that thing," said another. "It's a deathtrap."

Moments later, Morgan arrived on the scene. "If you let her escape, you won't get a penny out of me," he threatened.

The prospect of losing out on their share of the fortune was enough to make them quickly change their minds about crossing the bridge. Morgan stayed safely where he was, yelling orders.

Gemma wasn't sure who went first – she didn't dare look around again for fear of toppling into the rapids, but she felt the old ropes stretch and creak as the men followed her.

Suddenly, there was a loud snap from behind, and one of the two main side ropes broke, sending the bridge lurching violently to one side. Clinging to the remaining rope, Gemma managed to hang on and stop herself from falling.

The hunters panicked, shouting at each other to turn back before the second rope snapped, but they were too late. With a terrific ripping sound, the bridge tore apart, and three of the men plummeted into the watery depths below, swept away to their doom by the raging river.

Hanging by a thread, Gemma felt Tal's hand grab hers and pull her to safety.

The relief was almost overwhelming as her feet touched solid ground at last, and she turned to see the tattered remains of the bridge fluttering all the way down to the river.

"I expected a trip to the jungle to be exciting," she gasped breathlessly, "but I never imagined that it would be life threatening."

Tal frowned and looked across to where Morgan and his men were standing.

"The danger isn't over yet."

"You won't escape from me!" Morgan shouted at the top of his voice. "I'll hunt you down and make you pay for what you've done."

Taking a final look across at Morgan, Gemma turned away from him, ignoring his hateful threat.

She followed Tal through the jungle to a safe place he knew, and they stopped to rest under a huge, shady tree.

"It's so hot," she gasped, flopping down in an exhausted heap.

To quench their thirst, Tal picked some fruit which was growing nearby.

"Thanks," Gemma said gratefully, the juice running down her chin.

While she munched happily, she told Tal all about her time in Morgan's camp, and how he and his men planned to steal the jewelled statues.

"Any idea what we should do?" he asked.

"Well, we know they're heading for the temple, but if we can beat them to it then we could set a trap for them."

Tal looked thoughtful. "What sort of trap?"

Gemma pulled the map out of the pocket of her jeans. "I'm no expert on map reading, but I think this shows an area of dangerous, boggy ground around one side of the temple. What do you think?" She traced the area with her finger.

He confirmed that she was right. "That boggy ground is quicksand – to protect the temple from outsiders."

Folding the map, she put it back in her pocket. "With a bit of luck, they don't know about that, especially as I have their map," she grinned.

"That's all very well," he said, "but how will you manage to lure them into the trap?"

She shrugged her shoulders confidently. "Oh, I'll think of something once we get there."

Another thought occurred to Tal. "The temple is very well-hidden – it is possible that the hunters won't be able to find it."

That's not very likely, thought Gemma.

"As much as I dislike Morgan," she said, "he's obviously good at what he does. He's been to the temple once before, so I'm sure a man like him will find his way back again – with or without a map."

"You're probably right, but they'll have to take the long route around the river, which at least gives us more time to set the trap."

"How far are we from the temple?" she asked, gazing at the lush, tropical scenery which stretched for miles around.

He pointed to a hill on the horizon. "It's just beyond that ridge. If we start walking now, we'll arrive around sundown."

"Right, let's get going then!" Her voice sounded brave, but inside Gemma was a bundle of nerves. From the moment that she'd slipped the magic necklace around her neck, she'd come across a lot more in the jungle than she'd bargained for. She was glad that Tal was there to help, as she didn't relish the prospect of tackling Zack Morgan and his men on her own. But still she couldn't fight a niggling feeling of unease. Oh well, she thought to herself, the one thing that will keep me going is proving Ituxi wrong. I'm not 'only a girl' – I'll show him that girls can make good warriors, too.

"Something wrong?" Tal asked, interrupting her thoughts.

"Oh no, I was just hoping that luck will be on our side."

"Luck certainly isn't with the hunters," he remarked knowingly. "I wouldn't want to be Morgan. Anyone who steals the Jewel of the Jungle must fear the vengeance of the jaguar's third eye."

"Is that true?"

"According to the superstition, bad luck will follow Morgan through the jungle."

Gemma remembered what she had read about the mystic ruby in her big red book. "Is it true that the third eye gives the jaguar the power to see into the unknown?"

Tal nodded. "And whoever steals the ruby will never escape the jaguar's wrath."

6. A Hidden Doorway

By the time that Gemma and Tal arrived at the secret temple it was shrouded in darkness.

Hidden in the heart of the jungle, the temple towered upwards to the dark blue velvet sky. Camouflaged by leafy, spiralling vines, it merged naturally into its tropical surroundings. Had Gemma not known of its existence, she would never have guessed that it was there.

A magnificent stone jaguar guarded the entrance, its fiery-gold topaz eyes glinting in the moonlight. Maybe it was a trick of the light, but its eyes seemed to follow her every move. She had the weirdest sensation that it knew who she was.

The moon cast a silvery glow around the temple's silhouette, and long, dark shadows fell upon the ground. Although the air was calm, Gemma was sure that she could feel a chill breeze rustling through the leaves. Perhaps it's whispering my name, she thought, and then laughed at herself for being so silly. Nevertheless, a shiver ran down her spine.

"It's a bit spooky here at night," she said, looking at the eyes of the guardian cat which still seemed to be watching her.

Eventually, curiosity overcame her trepidation, and she walked over towards the statue to take a better look.

"Watch out for the quicksand!" Tal shouted cautiously. "If you fall in, you'll sink in seconds."

"I'll be careful."

Treading gently, Gemma moved closer to study the beautifully sculpted jaguar.

Up close, its topaz eyes looked so real. In the middle of its forehead was a large gap where the ruby – its mystic third eye – had been inset.

"The jaguar has guarded the temple for over a hundred years," Tal revealed. "In all that time, no one has ever dared steal the jewel."

"I'm sure we'll get it back," she said. Then, without thinking, she reached out and touched the jaguar's forehead, feeling the imprint of its third eye. Instantly, the ground began to tremble and she hurriedly drew her hand away, sensing that she had set something in motion.

She was right. The heavy wooden doors of the temple were firmly closed, but by touching the statue she had triggered a secret mechanism, causing them to slide open very slowly.

Gemma jumped back out of the way. The doors finally ground to a halt, and she peered into the vast space before her. A small, candle-like flame flickered dimly in the eerie darkness.

"You go first," she said, unsure of what was waiting for them.

Tal lifted an unlit torch from the wall inside the entrance. It was made from twigs bound tightly together. He dipped the tip of the torch into a large pot filled with a treacle-like oil, and then walked the short distance towards the small burning light. As soon as the tip of the torch touched the flame, it ignited, shedding a fiery glow around the temple.

"Here, take this." He handed her the lighted torch, then lit another for himself.

"Is someone else in here?" Gemma whispered to Tal.

"No, just you and me."

"So who lit the candle?" she questioned.

"It's an everlasting flame."

She breathed a sigh of relief. "For a moment I thought Morgan had beaten us to it."

"He shouldn't arrive for a while yet," Tal assured her. "Come on, I'll show you around."

Using his torch, he burned away an enormous spider's web that blocked their path.

Gemma shuddered. "What size of spider spins webs this big?"

"A giant one," he said, grinning. "The jungle is alive with them."

She cringed at the thought. Tal laughed, and walked on through the singed gap in the web, closely followed by Gemma.

Four steps led them down into a square where several small statues perched on a stone altar. Each statue was intricately carved into the shape of an animal and encrusted with precious gemstones.

Gemma held her torch aloft, the flame shining on the jewels. She could see sapphires, diamonds, rubies and emeralds sparkling in the light. Their dazzling beauty made her gasp in wonder.

"I'm not surprised that Morgan is willing to risk coming back here – there must be a fortune in jewels!"

"The statues are priceless and can never be replaced," Tal agreed. "We must do everything we can to stop the hunters getting their hands on them."

"Do you think your father will have spoken to the chief yet?"

"Yes, but Dandano may be angry with him for letting you escape and allowing me to go with you. He hates his commands being disobeyed."

"I was hoping Ituxi and Dandano might have arrived to help us fend off Morgan."

"They may still – we'll have to wait and see."

"Meanwhile it's just you and me, huh?"

He nodded. Beyond the ancient jewelled statues, a message was carved on the wall. Illuminating it with her torch, Gemma read it aloud. "Believe in the unbelievable and fate will guard your destiny." She turned to Tal. "What on earth does it mean?"

"It means that whatever happens, even if it's something incredible, we have to believe we can win in the end."

"Outside, I thought I heard my name whispered in the breeze, and I felt as if the stone jaguar knew who I was – now that's really unbelievable."

Tal didn't seem surprised. "This is sacred ground – strange things can happen here."

Suddenly, as if from nowhere, a black cloud of bats rose up and fluttered towards them. The noise of their rapidly beating wings and loud screeching cries reached a crescendo as they flew overhead, sending Gemma and Tal diving to the ground for cover.

Shielding her face with her hands, Gemma curled up into a protective ball and recoiled each time she felt the bats swooping past, their flapping wings brushing against her hair.

"I hate bats," she cringed, counting the seconds until the last of them had flown off through the open doorway.

Tal gave her a reassuring nudge before

getting to his feet. "They've gone."

Slowly she uncurled herself, peeking warily through her fingers to see them screeching into the night sky.

"My ears are ringing," she grumbled, rubbing them with her hands to soothe away the vibrating echoes.

Tal lifted Gemma's torch from where she had dropped it on the ground and handed it to her. "The light must have disturbed the bats."

"Or maybe something else rattled them," she suggested, walking towards the exit. "This really is a spooky place."

Her words were still hanging in the air, when – *whoosh!* The slab beneath her feet dropped open, catapulting her down a chute. The rush of air blew out her torch, and Gemma was left in total darkness.

She landed with a thud at the bottom of a pitch-black hole, knocking the breath from her lungs. In the darkness, she felt totally disorientated. Tentatively she felt her way around.

"Where am I?" she shouted, feeling nothing but cold, clammy stones.

"Gemma!" Tal shouted down to her. "Gemma, can you hear me?"

The light from his torch shone in the darkness, and she screwed up her eyes to adjust to the light. Then she opened them wide with horror – all around her were the indistinct shapes of stone coffins. She had fallen into an ancient tomb!

"Get me out of here!" she panicked. "Get me out – and quickly!"

"I'll try to find something that we can use to winch you out of there," Tal called. He ran off, taking the burning torch with him.

"Don't leave me in the dark," she shrieked frustratedly.

Tal ran back. "Stop shouting or you'll wake the dead!"

"That," said Gemma, "is simply not funny!" Anchoring his torch near the edge of the hole to give her some light, he ran off to find a rope.

"Hurry up!" she yelled from the bottom of the tomb, trying to forget what he had said earlier about the spiders that lived in the jungle.

Tal couldn't find a rope, but brought the

next best thing – a vine.

"Don't worry, Gemma, it's not a snake," he assured her, lowering one end down into the tomb and securing the other around the altar.

Right now, she didn't care what it was. Even if it was a python, she'd climb it rather than stay where she was.

"Can you climb the vine, or do you need me to haul you up?"

By the time his question echoed down to her, she was already hurriedly clambering up it.

Moments later, she was at the top. He pulled her to safety.

"That was one of the worst experiences of my entire life," Gemma gasped, shivering at the thought of it. "Bats, snakes and crocodiles are bad enough, but a jungle tomb is the absolute pits!

"Oh well, now I'm definitely in the mood to deal with Morgan. It's his fault we've had all these horrible things happening to us. If he hadn't stolen the ruby, we wouldn't be here in the first place. Come on, Tal, let's prepare the quicksand." She marched off, leaving him trailing in her wake.

"What's your plan?" he asked, once they were outside.

"To gather leaves and branches and lay them carefully over the quicksand."

"To disguise the trap?"

"Yes. Hopefully Morgan won't remember exactly where it is, especially as he doesn't have the map to remind him. Besides, when he sees me, he'll be so angry that he'll probably walk right into the trap. Once we've caught him, we'll force him to hand over the ruby before we pull him to safety."

Together they gathered lots of greenery and laid it in crisscross layers over the quicksand, to make it look like solid ground.

Sprinkling a few extra leaves on top, Gemma took a step back to judge their handiwork. "I'd never guess it was quicksand, would you?"

"No, and let's hope Morgan won't guess either – until it's too late."

"I wonder when he'll arrive," she mused,

having totally lost track of time.

There were steps leading up the outside of the temple to the flat-topped summit. "I'll climb up and take a look to see if the hunters are on their way," Tal said.

Gemma didn't want to be left standing alone in the creepy shadows. "Hang on, I'll go with you."

The steps rose at a steep angle. Gemma and Tal had to grasp hold of the vines which entwined the temple, to keep themselves steady while they climbed to the top.

"What a spectacular view," Gemma gasped, gazing at the moonlit jungle which stretched for miles around. Standing beneath the stars, she could see the distant hills, the winding rivers and lush green valleys. She breathed in the warm, exotic scent which wafted through the still air.

Tilting her head, she looked up at the sky. "The moon seems so close," she sighed. "I feel that I could almost reach out and touch it. And I've never seen so many stars," she added.

Tal agreed. "I love the Amazon – I never want to leave it."

"You're very lucky living in a place where you feel so happy," she said.

"Are you happy where you live?" Tal asked.

"Oh yes, of course, but I often wish I was somewhere else. I suppose that's why I use my magic necklaces to travel to places I could only dream about. But once I get there, I know my time is limited. Often I'd love to stay longer."

Just then, she saw Morgan and the hunters heading in their direction. "Here they come," she cried, feeling a surge of nervous excitement rush through her. It's now or never, she thought – knowing that the fate of the Jewel of the Jungle depended on her and Tal.

"Hurry," Gemma whispered, as they scrambled down the temple steps. "The hunters will be here soon."

7. The Jaguar's Revenge

Tal increased his pace, and together they descended to the ground. With only minutes to spare before the men arrived, they darted to their separate hiding places.

Gemma hid in the darkness behind the stone jaguar, her heart pounding anxiously as she crouched down out of sight. The statue sat in a corner on the right-hand side of the entrance, a short distance from the doors which Tal had closed securely. The quicksand lay straight ahead of her – and she was the bait in the trap.

Nearby, Tal disappeared into the shadows, invisible as the hunters approached the temple.

The men's voices sounded gruff, disturbing the calm of the night air. Gemma shivered with fear and anticipation. "Keep a lookout for any sign of trouble," Morgan ordered, telling several of his men to guard the perimeter of the temple. "And search the bushes for that troublesome girl and the boy who's with her."

From her hiding place, Gemma saw the men scatter in all directions, leaving Morgan, Jarrett and Deakin standing by themselves.

Remembering Tal's advice, she blended into the shadows and peered through half-closed eyes, in case they glinted in the light.

"The statues are inside," said Morgan. "Find them! Then let's get going."

The two men strode towards the entrance. For a moment, Gemma held her breath, fearing that they were going to step into the quicksand, but they missed it by a fraction.

Morgan stayed where he was, glancing around, as if expecting the Shadow People to jump out of the darkness and fight him for possession of the treasures.

"The doors are locked," Jarrett grumbled, pounding and pulling at them.

Deakin brushed him aside. "Stand back

and let me have a go." Putting his shoulder against the doors, he repeatedly tried to force them apart.

"It's no use," he said finally. "They won't budge."

"Check round the back," Morgan ordered. "See if there's another way in."

Jarrett and Deakin headed off, leaving Morgan alone.

While he waited, he took the ruby from his pocket, held it up to the moonlight and admired its precious cut and gleaming rich red colour.

Gemma watched his every move, poised ready to snare him when the moment was right. Her pulse was quickening by the second. She had never felt so tense.

Nearby, she caught a glimpse of Tal signalling to her that help was on its way. Then he vanished into the night again.

Her eyes flicked back to Morgan, who was still fascinated by the dazzling beauty of the jewel.

She sensed that it was time to make her move.

Taking a deep breath, she stood up from

behind the jaguar. "The ruby doesn't belong to you, Zack Morgan."

He spun around, and from beneath the brim of his black hat, his eyes narrowed angrily. "I might have guessed you'd be here," he snarled.

Furiously, he stomped towards her, heading straight for the quicksand.

Gemma clung to the jaguar, not daring to move.

"I warned you – I'll make you pay for stealing my map," he raged. "You'll wish you'd never come here with your fancy ideas! You and your explorations! You'll be sorry you ever – "

His threat was cut short as he stepped into the quicksand, sinking instantly up to his waist in the treacherous bog.

"Aaagh!" he cried, frantically reaching out with one hand to save himself, while clutching the ruby in the other. "Help me!"

Gemma moved closer. "All you have to do is give me the ruby and then I'll pull you free."

"Never!" he shouted defiantly, sinking further into the quicksand, which was sucking him down into oblivion. "The jewel is mine."

"It isn't yours. It belongs to the tribe and you should never have stolen it in the first place. I found your logbook and I know everything."

"You tricked me," he gasped. "There never was a gold mine, was there?"

"No," Gemma confessed.

His face was etched with fear as he slid further down, still managing to hold the ruby aloft, but struggling desperately to escape.

Quickly glancing around, Gemma wondered why none of the hunters had rushed to his aid. Surely they must have heard him shouting for help? Where were they all? And where, more importantly, was Tal?

The quicksand swallowed Morgan deeper into its fathomless depths.

"This is your last chance," she warned him. "Give me the ruby!"

By now, his rage had turned to terror. "Throw me a vine," he gasped, as the quicksand squeezed his chest, making it difficult for him to breathe. "Then I'll give you the jewel."

"No way!" she bluffed. In her heart, no matter how much she hated Morgan, she couldn't let him perish.

As the seconds ticked past, he began to tire, hardly able to hold the gem.

She realised that he was running out of time, but was just too stubborn to let go of the ruby, so she leaned over and snatched it from his weakened grasp.

Morgan was powerless to stop her.

"Here, grab hold of this," she said, thrusting a strong vine into his outstretched palm.

Clutching tightly to the lifeline, he began to drag himself free.

Gemma didn't plan on hanging around, and ran off with the jewel in search of Tal. Where was everyone?

From far behind the temple, she heard men's voices raised in anger; it sounded as if a fight was taking place.

Gemma realised that the Shadow People had arrived to fend off the hunters, and her heart leaped. Last time, the tribe had been unprepared to defend their temple, but this time they were ready – and she knew who would win if it came to a fight to protect their sacred treasures. The hunters wouldn't stand a chance. No wonder Morgan's men hadn't rushed to his rescue; they were too busy taking care of themselves.

"Gemma!" Tal shouted, hurrying to her side. "Are you all right?"

"Yes," she said. "And I've got the jewel." Triumphantly she held it up to the moonlight.

Suddenly, Tal noticed the black hat lying in the middle of their trap, and suspected the worst. "Where's Morgan? Did the quicksand get him?"

"Let's just say he had a narrow escape," she said, smiling. "But we've got the ruby."

"Our warriors chased away the other hunters – this time for good. Quite a few of them are badly wounded, which should serve as a warning never to come back."

A huge sigh of relief overwhelmed Gemma, and she knew that her adventure was happily complete. "Hopefully you've seen the last of Zack Morgan."

"I doubt if he'll ever return...he dared to steal the jaguar's third eye, and it will wreak its own revenge on him. It's a long way back through the jungle – he will never escape the jaguar's wrath."

At that moment, Ituxi and Dandano walked towards them, smiling at Gemma.

Ituxi was the first to thank her. "You're an amazing girl. We owe you a great debt of gratitude."

"I couldn't have done it without Tal's help," she said, grateful to her new friend for all his support.

Dandano stepped forward. "We would be honoured if you would stay here with us."

Sadly, she refused. "I wish I could, but it's time for me to go."

Taking one last, lingering look at the precious ruby, she handed it to the chief.

"You will always be remembered by the Shadow People," Dandano said proudly, then he turned and walked away, disappearing into the darkness.

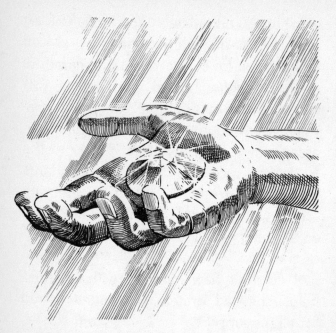

Ituxi looked deep into her eyes. "Are you sure you can't stay a while longer?"

She shook her head. "No, I'm running out of magic."

He seemed to understand. "I want you to have this," he said, giving her one of his carved wooden necklaces. "It will bring you good luck."

Gratefully accepting his gift, Gemma slipped it over her head. The beads were heavier and longer than her own.

Then she remembered the map. Pulling it from the pocket of her jeans, she handed it to the medicine man. "This is Morgan's map. Destroy it so that no one else can discover where the temple is hidden."

He nodded solemnly.

Tal was strangely quiet, resigned to the fact that he would never see Gemma again. She turned to face him, knowing that she had one last thing to do before she left.

"I'd like you to accept my magic necklace, Tal."

Unfastening the beads, the whole world seemed to spin around, faster and faster, and Gemma felt as if she was falling. Then, with a bump, she landed on her bed. The thunderstorm still raged outside, and there was a soft purring sound coming from underneath the bed.

Blinking to adjust to her familiar surroundings, the first thing she noticed was the big red book lying open just where she'd left it.

Moving over for a closer look, she sat wn to study the open pages. There's something different about the picture of the jaguar, she thought. The animal's topaz eyes stared out from the page, as though it was watching her, but something had changed. She racked her brains to remember what it was.

Suddenly it dawned on her – the ruby was inset on its forehead! Its mystic third eye was back where it belonged, instead of the hole where the gem had been.

"How amazing," she murmured. Then she read the story beside the picture – that had changed, too!

"The jaguar's third eye, a precious gemstone known as the Jewel of the Jungle, went missing in 1933, but was later found and returned safely to the Shadow People tribe."

"Wow!" she gasped, with amazement and pride.

Flopping backwards on to her pillow, she gazed up at the ceiling, reflecting on her wonderful Amazon adventure. It was all so unreal. Ituxi's beads were real enough, though. Carefully, she took them off and rummaged to find her jewell box. Geronimo purred contentedly as Gemma picked him up from his hiding place and cuddled him. Then she placed the Amazon necklace gently in the box, alongside the magic ones of her secret collection.

Stifling a weary yawn, she realised how tired she was. Although not a moment had passed since she travelled back in time to 1933, she'd been running and climbing through the jungle for almost two days. Exhaustion was catching up with her.

She decided that it was time for bed, but not before she'd popped downstairs to the fridge for a long, cool drink.

Walking into the kitchen, Mum said, "How's your History project going? You've been beavering away up there for hours!"

Homework? Homework was the last thing on Gemma's mind! "Oh, I've nearly sorted it out, I think," she fibbed. "But I keep getting distracted."